MW00353847

The Demon King
and Other Festival Folktales of China

The Demon King

and Other Festival Folktales of China

Retold by Carolyn Han

Translated by Jay Han

Illustrated by Li Ji

A KOLOWALU BOOK

University of Hawai‘i Press

Honolulu

Library of Congress Cataloging-in-Publication Data

Han, Carolyn, 1941–

The demon king and other festival folktales of China / retold by

Carolyn Han ; translated by Jay Han ; illustrated by Li Ji.

p.   cm.

Translated from Chinese.

ISBN 0–8248–1907–9 (acid-free paper)

1. Tales—China.   2. Festivals—China.   3. China—Ethnology.

II. Title.

GR335.H363   1995

398.2'0951—dc20   95–16064

CIP

University of Hawai'i Press books are printed on acid-free paper

and meet the guidelines for permanence and durability of the

Council on Library Resources

Design by Paula Newcomb

Dedication

WITH heartfelt appreciation to all my friends who have accompanied me on the mountains above the clouds and who have walked with me in the misty valleys below the clouds. My journey has been made easier because of you.

To Carol Soderlund, who visited me while I lived in China and validated my oftentimes crazy experience: for her continuous love, friendship, and encouragement throughout the years.

To Julia Tao, who has been a bridge between East and West: for her invaluable help in translating my Chinese correspondence and for her honesty, positive spirit, and unconditional love.

To David, my son, who remains my constant connection with China.

Contents

Preface

CHINA, with its tremendous population of over one billion two hundred million, is a country of incredible diversity. The majority of its people, 93 percent, are Han (ethnic Chinese), while the remaining 7 percent make up the fifty-five national minority groups that live within the borders. These vast numbers of people account for the immense variation in language, custom, religion, art forms, food, dress, and festivals.

Throughout the world people celebrate different festivals and honor different dates, but our celebrations are a universal connection that we all share. These observances reflect who we were, who we are, and who we will become. Celebrating festivals gives people the opportunity to reenact rituals, to prepare and eat special foods, to wear traditional clothing, to play and sing distinct music—they connect us with our deepest selves so that we may form an unbroken link with our past to ensure our future and possibly our immortality.

Many festivals have combined several different celebrations to form one. Their stories, or legends, of how they originated have been obscured with time. Other festivals have origins that can be traced to their very beginnings, and they have not changed over the thousands of years. These accounts, or sometimes folktales, that surround the celebrations tell us about the people's values, beliefs, customs, religions, and histories.

When we listen to the stories, legends, and folktales and learn more about who the minority people are and what they believe, we may begin to understand them. We learn to respect their differences and possibly see that we share some similarities. Ultimately we learn that we all share a very small planet, inhabited by many interesting and unique people. As we learn about other people, and why they celebrate their festivals, we are encouraged to ask questions about our own celebrations. In this way we may explore our past and see ourselves from new perspectives.

In 1985 I began learning about the many national minority people, as they are called, in China. Before living in China I had only a vague understanding of the minority groups that reside in this diverse country. For the three years I lived and worked in Sichuan and Yunnan, I came into daily contact with Bai, Dai, Dulong, Hani, Miao, Naxi, Xizang (Tibetan), Zhuang, and many other minority peoples. They were all different from the Han Chinese and different from each other.

Their differences intrigued me and I wanted to know more. But, given China's tremendous population and rich diversity, where could I begin? As with all learning, the first step starts with a question. With questions come answers. Most of the fifty-five distinct minority groups living in China celebrate festivals unique to each group. If I could learn about their festivals, then I might gain some clues about the people themselves.

My first year at Chongqing University in Sichuan was coming to a close, and I still needed to know more about the minority nationalities. How could I leave when I was just beginning to find some answers? After throwing the *I Ching*—and after my application to teach English at Yunnan Institute of the Nationalities in the capital city of Kunming was accepted—I stayed in China another two years. Teaching in Yunnan gave me access to students from twenty-two of the different minority groups that inhabit this remote southwestern province of China. With this contact came the opportunity to attend festivals and learn more about these fascinating people.

This book is a collection of four festival stories translated from *The*

Folklore and Customs in China.* Like all good stories passed down from generation to generation, they can be told and retold in endless ways. In my retelling of these folktales I have tried to remain close to the original translations, but because I am a storyteller I have taken some poetic license. These legends from the Dai, Xizang, Miao, and Hani tell us how or why each festival originated. These four stories were chosen because they are entertaining and reflect the values, beliefs, life-styles, and customs of the nationalities. They were also selected because the festivals can still be seen in China today and outsiders may take part in them. Although these minority groups celebrate many festivals, the four presented here are unique and important to each group's identity.

The group identity of a national minority is also associated with the land area it occupies. Topographical diversity is evident throughout China's gigantic land mass. China's enormous expanse of land includes the highest mountain, the lowest desert, and everything else in between. Over centuries many of the minority groups have been pushed from the north to the south and southwest. Numerous groups now reside in this south-western section of China. Two of the stories are from Yunnan, or "South of the Clouds" as it is known. The Dai live in the southern section of Yunnan in Xishuangbanna and Dehong. The Hani live high in the mountainous regions of Yunnan along the Hong He, or "Red River." The Xizang story is set on the "Roof of the World" in the capital city of Lhasa. Most Xizang live on this far western edge, and large numbers also live in Yunnan, Sichuan, Qinghai, and Gansu. The Miao story is from Guizhou where many live, but a large population of Miao reside in Yunnan and Sichuan. The four minority groups are concentrated mainly in these areas, but some live in the surrounding regions.

*The stories were translated from: *Zhongguo min jian feng su chuan shuo: Yunnan* (The folklore and customs in China: Yunnan). Kunming: Yunnan renmin chuban she, 1985.

Distribution of Some Minority Groups in Southwestern China

XIZANG (TIBET)

Lhasa

Chengdu

SICHUAN

YUNNAN

GUIZHOU

Guiyang

Dehong

Kunming

Xishuangbanna

Dai

Miao

Xizang

Hani

It has been my good fortune to have lived and worked in China. For China changed my life. Living in China also gave me the opportunity to meet Jay Han and Li Ji, both of whom worked hard to make this book a reality. Jay Han researched the stories, worked on the translations, and explained the complex cultural nuances. Li Ji, with his remarkable talent and profound understanding of the minority people, has given life to the book with his colorful, imaginative illustrations.

My deepest respect goes to Iris M. Wiley, executive editor of the University of Hawai'i Press, for her generous spirit, support, and suggestions. Without her this book would still be "beyond the clouds." A special thanks to Sally Serafim, managing editor, for her gentle but constant coaxing to get this book "out of the clouds." My profound appreciation to Cheng Jaiho, a guardian angel; thank you for all your help.

May these tales increase your appreciation of China and give you the opportunity to know more about the Dai, Xizang, Miao, and Hani—four fascinating groups of people that add to the abundant diversity and uniqueness of the "Middle Kingdom." My hope is that this book will also inspire you to ask questions about your own people, your own traditions, your own cultures, and your own festivals.

May you never stop asking questions. Or finding answers.

The Demon King of the Dai

THE STORY OF THE WATER SPLASHING FESTIVAL

Long, long ago, in Xishuangbanna, a far-off southwestern section of China, there lived a group of people known as the Dai. In those early days the Dai had a cruel and violent ruler who was hated by all the people. This fierce demon had descended from the sixteenth level of heaven and brought with him incredible supernatural powers. He did whatever he wanted—took whatever he wanted—with never a thought or concern for those in his kingdom. If he wanted rice and crops, he took them. If he wanted land and livestock, he took them. If he wanted slaves, he took them. This greedy king was never satisfied. He was known throughout the land as the "Demon King."

The gentle and kind Dai were defenseless against this terrifying ruler. Nothing in the world could destroy him. Water could not drown him. Fire could not burn him. Spears and swords could not penetrate him. He was indestructible! The Dai had to serve this dreadful tyrant because they feared his mystical powers and what he might do to them if they ever refused or resisted.

In keeping with his vile reputation, the Demon King stole six of the most beautiful Dai women to be his wives. Each woman had been taken from her family without their consent, and each of them hated him and wanted revenge. Nevertheless, they were helpless against his power.

The greedy Demon King was never content with what he had and always wanted more. His inability to be satisfied made him search for yet

another wife. But after weeks and weeks of hunting through all the villages in Xishuangbanna, he still had not found a new bride. His frustration and his anger grew. The Dai began to worry.

The Demon King became so enraged because he could not find a new wife that he decided to take revenge on his people. He began planning his retaliation, but first he needed to return to the palace. To return he had to cross the Lancang River by way of a swaying bamboo bridge. While he was on the bridge, he saw an enchanted being walking toward him. A princess. Truly the most magnificent woman he had ever seen was directly in his path. She was dressed in a lavender, close-fitting, long-sleeve top and a long, wrapped skirt patterned with circles. A thin, woven, silver belt held her skirt around her slender waist. Her shiny black hair was pulled back from her face and fashioned into a loose coil on the side. She did not raise her head to look at the Demon King as they passed, but he could see that her dark, almond-shaped eyes sparkled. Her beauty was beyond compare. Instantly he knew that he had found a treasure—his seventh wife.

At once he ordered her to be captured, and Nan Zhongbu, as she was called, was immediately taken to the palace. An auspicious date was set for the wedding. To ensure a prosperous, long marriage, the longest day of the year was chosen.

Soon after their wedding the Demon King realized his new wife not only possessed the most captivating beauty but also was the most intelligent of all the wives. Because of her outer and inner beauty she soon became his favorite.

She, like the other six wives, hated the Demon King, but, unlike the others, she did not let her true feelings be known. She pretended to be fond of him, to attend to him, to please him in every way. Her pretense was so believable that he never knew how she really felt.

One evening Nan Zhongbu decided to test the Demon King when he

was in an unusually good mood and said, "My lord, everyone knows that you have unlimited powers and that nothing can harm you." Continuing her false flattery, she added, "You are strong and I feel very safe with you. If you could grant me one wish, it would be that we could live together forever."

Listening to her words, but not knowing they were lies, the Demon King was delighted by them and decided to tell her his secret. A secret he had never told anyone before. "I too am vulnerable," he confessed. "I have one fatal flaw. One flaw that no one must know."

"How can that be?" she questioned. "My lord, you are all-mighty and all-powerful. Surely, you are teasing me."

"If you promise never to tell, I'll confide my secret to you," he said. "But you must promise."

Stepping closer to the Demon King, Nan Zhongbu assured him she could be trusted with such a secret. He leaned even closer to his wife and whispered in her ear, "If someone would use a hair from my head to cut into my neck, I would be destroyed."

That very same night the seventh wife made sure the Demon King had an extra cup of sweet rice wine before he retired. When he was fast asleep, she plucked a hair from his head and with it she cut into his neck. His big head fell off and dropped to the floor. "Aiya!" she shouted. "It is done! I can tell the others!"

Word of the Demon King's death spread quickly throughout Xishuangbanna. Everyone was thrilled that his terrible reign had come to an end. They planned parties. They rejoiced. Now their lives would be happy and peaceful because they would no longer be tortured or threatened by the brutal king.

But alas! Wherever the head rolled—disaster followed! If it rolled on the ground, the ground caught on fire. If it rolled into the river, the river water boiled and all the fish died. When the Dai tried to bury the head

under the ground, the stench was overpowering and nothing grew. Nan Zhongbu felt she had no other choice but to hold the head with her hands so that it would not bring grief and disaster to her people. Day and night, night and day, she held the head in her hands until she became horribly exhausted. Seeing her plight, the six other wives felt compassion toward her, and each decided to take a turn holding the Demon King's head. All seven women took turns and passed the head from one to the other. When the wives rested, they refreshed themselves by pouring and splashing water on each other. With the splashing water they also washed away the blood stains and the revolting smell that came from the severed head.

The seven women thus took on the enormous task of tending to the head so that the other Dai would not be burdened. In celebration and to commemorate the seven brave women who were ready to suffer for the others, and in thanks for killing the Demon King, the Dai people held a festival. One of the festival rituals was that people splashed water on each other, not only to imitate the seven Dai women washing off the Demon King's blood but also to show their respect and shower blessings.

People in Xishuangbanna and Dehong continue to this day to hold a Water Splashing Festival, retell the story of the Demon King's death, and honor the seven courageous women. Each year the Dai pour, splash, and sometimes drench each other in memory of Nan Zhongbu and the six wives who sacrificed themselves for the good of the Dai people.

HOW THE WATER SPLASHING FESTIVAL IS
NOW CELEBRATED

THE largest concentrations of Dai are in Xishuangbanna and Dehong, the southernmost part of Yunnan, and each year they celebrate a Water Splashing Festival. The festival falls on the Dai New Year, and it comes between the twenty-fourth and twenty-sixth day of the sixth month on the Dai calendar, which is approximately mid-April on the Western calendar.

In recent years the festival has been open to outsiders so that guests from many lands may attend and take part. The flights from Kunming to Yunjinghong (meaning the "City of Dawn" in Dai) are reserved months in advance. Even though visitors are now welcome to be a part of the festivities, the Dai maintain their age-old traditions. Year after year the story of the Demon King is retold as a part of the festival. And like all retold stories, it can be told in many ways. Sometimes the story contains seven wives and sometimes twelve, but water splashing is a consistent theme.

Pouring and splashing water at the New Year celebration also has a religious component based on the Dai belief in Hinayana Buddhism and its custom of washing the statues of Buddha with perfumed water. Using water is an ancient religious practice in many lands—several other Southeast Asian countries have similar festivals—and it often represents a washing away of the old and a welcoming in of the new. The New Year's celebration is held to bring good luck, happiness, and prosperity for the coming year.

A dragon-boat race is held on the first day of the Dai Water Splashing

Festival, and all day long the villages compete against one another. The Lancang (Mekong) River comes alive with the colorfully painted wooden boats. Uniquely carved dragon heads at the prow and curled dragon tails at the stern make the boats floating works of art. The crew, dressed in bright colors and wearing red cloth tied around their heads like turbans, complete the wondrous scene. While rhythmically rowing their boats, they chant loudly to keep time with the oars. The people on the riverbanks encourage the teams with wild cheering and pounding on the *xiangjiaogu*, which are drums shaped like elephant legs. At the end of the races, both the winners and the losers join together to sing, dance, and feast in celebration.

On the second day of the festival the water splashing begins. Everyone joins in and enjoys this festivity. The older generation gently sprinkle their friends with scented water by dipping a small branch into a hand-held bucket, and the exuberant younger people drench each other by throwing the entire contents of filled buckets and basins. Supposedly the more water you splash, the more sincere the blessing. Everybody gets wet—no one in Xishuangbanna or Dehong is dry!

On the third day of the celebration the Dai light firecrackers to scare away the evil spirits, and the "pop-pop-pop" can be heard far into the night. They also shoot off homemade rockets made of bamboo tubes filled with gunpowder. These rockets fly through the air and explode, releasing small gifts. The Dai, and now the visitors, rush to pick up a keepsake, because to get a prize means to have good luck for the coming year.

All three days the villages are alive with activities—eating special foods, meeting old and new friends, and singing and dancing. Music from the *lusheng* (a wind instrument made of bamboo reeds) and the *xiangjiaogu* accompanies the spirited crowd. Their religious belief in Hinayana Buddhism plays an important role in Dai life, and it can be seen in the Masked Dances that are performed during the festival to scare away the evil spirits.

Peacocks for the Dai symbolize good luck, and there is a special dance that mimics the graceful and intricate movements of this elegant bird. The festival is the best time to see the stunning dance performed. Because not everyone has the ability to execute the controlled movements of the peacock dance, the Dai also hold group dances so that everyone may participate. People form lines and lines of concentric circles, swaying their bodies in rhythm to the music and walking forward and waving their hands gracefully in the air. The friendly Dai encourage visitors to dance and to join the holiday spirit.

This occasion also affords a time for young men and women to get together. An age-old courtship ritual known as the "Dui Bao" is held during the festival. *Dui* means "to throw" and *bao* means "bag" or "pouch." For the Dai the *bao* is a colorfully embroidered triangular pouch with bright yarn tassels at its corners. During this happy event, prospective couples line up facing each other and begin throwing the colorful *bao* back and forth. The couples who are interested in forming a friendship continue throwing the *bao,* stepping closer with every toss.

Each year in Xishuangbanna and Dehong the Water Splashing Festival is held, giving the Dai people the opportunity to come together, to celebrate their age-old customs, to send out the old year, and to welcome in the new. As visitors are warmly welcomed, this spirited festival is definitely one to experience—but be prepared to be drenched.

Dr. Yuto and the Wild Rat Star

THE STORY OF THE XIZANG BATHING FESTIVAL

EACH summer a bright star appears in the southeastern portion of the sky, high, high in the heavens above Lhasa, or "God's Place," the capital of Xizang (Tibet). The "Wild Rat Star," as the Xizang call it, shines only seven nights each year. During the star's bright but brief reign they celebrate the Bathing Festival. The festival began long, long ago and no one can remember its exact date, but no one has forgotten why it began.

On top of the "Roof of the World," as Xizang is known, there once lived a brilliantly gifted doctor by the name of Yuto Yundangongbu. This distinguished doctor had the ability to cure any and all illnesses. In fact, his reputation for curing disease was so well known that King Chisungdezhan wanted Dr. Yuto to be his court physician and to serve only him.

Of course Dr. Yuto did as the king ordered and lived in the palace to assist the royal family. But even though he lived in the palace, he never forgot or neglected the country people. While collecting roots and wild herbs from the mountainsides, he would visit the sick in the rural villages that dot the stark, mountainous landscape. After listening to their symptoms and examining them, he would concoct just the right potions to cure their ailments. Being a true healer, Dr. Yuto did not charge for his medicine. He was content with seeing his people well and knowing he had helped.

One year a terrible plague broke out. It swept through the highlands from mountain to mountain until many Xizang people suffered and eventually died from the dreaded disease. Soon whole families were wiped out—then whole villages. When the news of the ghastly epidemic reached Dr. Yuto, he set out in search of a cure. He traveled high up the towering, snow-covered mountains and deep into the remote, wooded valleys to gather the rare medicinal herbs necessary for the treatments. As he crossed and crisscrossed the steep mountains, he dispensed his special medicines. The potions worked like magic, and soon the sick and dying were well again. Dr. Yuto's reputation spread among the Xizang people until everyone called him the "King of Pharmacy."

Year after year the kind doctor continued to cure his people with the medicinal, almost mystical, herbs. Even though he could no longer climb the highest peaks or descend into the deepest valleys to gather roots and herbs, he still worked hard to heal his people. With added age, however, Dr. Yuto gradually slowed down. Then slower, slower, slower, until he finally died.

When another plague broke out after his death, the Xizang people realized how great was their loss. They needed him even more, because this time a worse epidemic swept across the land. Not only were people dying, but also the animals were falling in the fields.

All the able-bodied Xizang flew their rainbow-colored, triangular prayer flags tied to long streamers that rippled in the wind. The kaleidoscope of colorful pennants fluttered outside the temples and on the mountaintops, asking for blessings from above. At all hours the sound of whirling, twirling prayer wheels could be heard, echoing through the streets and carrying prayers toward heaven. The devout Xizang made offerings—especially to the Goddess of Mercy—to ask for blessings. Perfumed incense burned on altars and the glow from the yak butter candles shown brightly from the temple windows. The holy temples were surrounded by faithful worshipers slowly walking clockwise around the grounds from morning to night. No matter what the Xizang did, nothing helped. People and animals died.

Late one night, during the early part of the seventh month on the Xizang calendar, a devout Xizang woman who was tending her animals on the mountain fell into a deep sleep because of a high fever. While she slept on the wildflower-covered ground she had a vivid dream—a dream so real that she was sure Dr. Yuto appeared to her and said, "Tomorrow you will see a bright star in the southeast sky. When the brilliant star twinkles and shines, go to the river to bathe."

As soon as the radiant star appeared in the night sky the very next evening, the woman, who believed in dreams, went to the river. She inched her way slowly into the cold, crystal-clear water, and immediately her fever dropped, her mind relaxed, her body healed. She was cured. The story of the miraculous healing quickly spread across the land. Within days everyone knew about the curative powers of the bright star shining above the water, and people came from all over Xizang to be healed.

The people believe that the bright star is Dr. Yuto. They believe that he transformed himself into a star and shines down from the heavens to bless them and cure their diseases. From on high Dr. Yuto had looked down on his people and watched them suffer as bodhisattvas have done since the beginning of time. His frustration increased because he could not return to earth to help them, so he decided to transform himself into a star—the Wild Rat Star. But the King of Heaven allows him only one week to change himself into a star and help his people. Since that time long, long ago, Dr. Yuto changes himself into the Wild Rat Star for only seven days each year and shines down from heaven to heal his people. If you are anywhere near Xizang during the summer be sure to look in the southeastern sky to see the Wild Rat Star smiling down on you. When you find the brightest star on the horizon, you will have found Dr. Yuto. Go at once to the closest river to ask for his blessing, and join the throngs of people celebrating in the healing water.

IN Xizang, Yunnan, Sichuan, and the surrounding areas, the Bathing Festival is held each summer when the Wild Rat Star (probably Canopus) appears in the southeastern sky. People camp on the mountainsides along the riverbanks and bathe in the water in order to receive Dr. Yuto's blessings and be healed.

Summer is an ideal time of the year to bathe outside because the temperatures are warmer and the river water much cleaner. In winter the water is frozen or too cold owing to the ice and snow high in the mountains. In the spring, when the ice and glaciers begin to melt, the rushing torrents of water pick up soil and rocks and carry them along, making the river water very dirty and not suitable for bathing.

When the star shines during the summer, families go to the nearby rivers and streams. During this time the Xizang also wash their clothes, and the banks alongside the water's edge are lined with quilts, mattresses, felt robes, pants, and rainbow-colored aprons spread out in every direction, resembling weathered Xizang prayer flags.

In celebration, many families bring their decorated tents and camp on the hillsides beside the rivers for the full seven days. Meals are cooked outside on open fires, and the Xizang food staples of buttered and salted tea and *tsampa,* roasted barley flour, are easy and ideal foods to prepare. Buttered and salted tea is used for drinking. It is also blended with roasted barley flour in a wooden bowl by using the fingers of the right hand. The mealy mixture is shaped into elongated balls, passed around like snack food, and eaten with the fingers. Most Xizang eat several small meals a day, instead of two or three large meals, to give themselves the constant energy they need at the high elevations. Many Xizang have restricted diets because they live at such high elevations where only limited crops grow. Most live at elevations over one mile, and many live higher than four miles above sea level. Because of the high altitudes and the cold temperatures, Xizang has a short growing season. Limited food includes barley, peas, buckwheat, lamb, and yak meat. The shaggy yak also supplies milk, cheese, butter, and yogurt.

During the Bathing Festival, meals are often taken together with old and new friends. Young people get together to "Throw Handkerchiefs" and "Snatch Hats"—both games of courtship. When the day comes to a close, after bathing and washing, the Xizang light fires, tell stories, sing songs, perform dances, and look up at the night sky to say a special "thank you" to Dr. Yuto, who continues to shine down on them year after year.

The Feather—A Miao Love Story

THE STORY OF THE LUSHENG FESTIVAL

AGES and ages ago, in a remote part of Guizhou high in the cloud-covered village of Zhounai, there lived a lovely young maiden by the name of Ahwong. She not only was breathtaking to behold, but also was considered the "Pearl of Purity and Piety" by the Miao.

Ahwong's jewel-like qualities endeared her to all people and to all living things. Animals, both large and small, joined her as she walked through the forest. The sound of her singing could cause the birds to stop midflight and sit with her as she worked on her embroidery alongside the bubbling brook.

"Everyone Wears Flowers" is an expression that describes the Miao people's love for their colorfully embroidered clothing. Ahwong's needle-work was famous among the Miao. Her deft handiwork even fooled the bees into believing that her artful creations were a part of nature. She was gifted and clever, a treasure for all to admire.

Admiration for Ahwong came not only from the good villagers but also from a fierce, brutal Chicken Demon who lived in a craggy cave high on the mountain. This menacing demon took whatever he wanted, and now he decided he wanted Ahwong for his bride.

In the past the evil demon often used his wicked wizardry to bring destruction upon the Miao. He set tornado-like winds in motion to tear the crops from the ground. Changing himself into a fierce tiger, he destroyed their food supply by killing the livestock. Transformed into a wolf, he stole Miao children and carried them off to his cave. The villagers never knew what form the hateful demon might take or what he might do. But the Miao were at his mercy because he could not be stopped.

Using black magic, the demon tried to win Ahwong's hand in marriage. First he changed himself into a rich merchant and brought her many precious and expensive gifts. Using the sweetest words to flatter her and her father, the demon asked to marry Ahwong. But her father objected because he listened to his intuition and was not fooled. Next the demon changed himself into a scholar and pretended to be gentle and sensitive and to possess a good heart, but Ahwong could see through his disguise. She, too, listened to her intuition and was not fooled.

His failure to win her heart so angered the Chicken Demon that he decided to take her by force. At once he compelled the north winds to blow, and soon the roofs soared from the houses, scattering the terrified people to the four cardinal points. While the people panicked and ran for shelter, the demon seized the opportunity to take Ahwong to his cave.

As soon as the people realized what had happened, they began circling the mountain, holding their blazing torches high in the air. Their only hope was to scare away the demon and free Ahwong. When that did not work, the best archers were called from the neighboring mountain villages. Round after round of arrows left their bows and flew through the air, but, try as they might, the teams of courageous archers could not kill the Chicken Demon.

Hideous sounds came from the demon in hopes of scaring the people away, but still they circled the mountain. He commanded hundreds of brass gongs to sound, clashing and clapping until the thunderous noise made the people deaf, but still they did not leave. When the demon flapped his giant, outstretched wings to fight off the arrows, he sent sand and rocks flying into their eyes, blinding them, but still they stayed.

With his powerful wings he created a fierce wind and cast the arrows

in the opposite direction, almost hitting the villagers. But the demon could not deflect all the arrows, and a few came very close to his neck. He was terrified, because if an arrow hit his neck, he would die. For protection he withdrew back into his cave.

A fearless hunter, Maosa, happened to be nearby hunting bears when he heard the news about the Chicken Demon capturing Ahwong. Maosa was thought to be the best archer in all of Guizhou, maybe the best in the world. According to rumor, he could shoot an arrow with such precision that he could place the second arrow on the end of the first. Given Maosa's outstanding reputation as both an experienced marksman and a compassionate person, the villagers were sure he would help.

The villagers were right. Soon Maosa arrived at the foot of the mountain. They explained what had happened and just before midnight he began his climb up the backside of the rocky slope to seek out the demon and free Ahwong. After scaling the vertical stone cliffs, he finally reached the top and hid in the pitch-black night. By the filtered rays of first light, he saw the enormous white Chicken Demon sitting high on a rock outcropping outside the entrance to its cave, with red talons outstretched and ready to tear him to pieces. While Maosa looked around for a glimpse of Ahwong, the demon taunted him over and over again with horrible, screeching curses. The demon bird never let up his violent threats, but in the far-off distance Maosa also heard a soft crying—a weeping sound carried on the gentle wind.

Quickly stepping forward and taking careful aim, Maosa released his golden arrow with the force of a thunderbolt. He hit his mark. The arrow entered the demon's neck, and before he could transform himself into another form, he plummeted to earth. With only one shot from Maosa's bow, the demon lay dead. Maosa waited and listened again for the faint crying, but the wind and the sound had stopped. He searched frantically for Ahwong, calling her name over and over, but he could not find her.

Feeling dreadfully disappointed, Maosa finally had to abandon his search and leave the mountain. But before he left he plucked a white feather from the Chicken Demon and carried it with him to commemorate the day.

When the demon had captured Ahwong, he knew that she might try to escape. He could not take the chance that she might flee, so he had placed on her a magic spell that caused her to sleep all day, and all night. Only at daybreak was she allowed to wake.

The following dawn Ahwong woke and ran from the cave into the early morning light. When she realized that she was all alone, she searched for the path that led down the rocky mountainside. After finding the narrow footpath, she continued along it until she met the villagers, who told her how Maosa slayed the demon and saved her life. They could not give her any details about the hunter except that when he left the mountain he had a brilliant white feather in his hat.

Ahwong wanted to know more about the brave hunter who had saved her life, but after a while she gave up hope of ever seeing him. Soon her sadness turned to despair, and before long she became very sick. Ahwong's health grew worse until finally she became so weak that her family realized it was only a matter of time until she would relinquish all hope and die.

Late one evening when Ahwong's mother and father were alone, her father said, "Our daughter is sure to die if we don't find the hunter. We have to find him!"

Ahwong's mother sighed. "It has already been so long. What can we do?"

"The New Year is coming and we can hold a festival—a *lusheng* competition," the father said. "We can invite all the Miao to the celebration to sing and dance and play the *lusheng*. I'm sure when the hunter hears about it he will return to our village."

Ahwong's father was considered a very clever man by the villagers. "It will work," he assured himself. "It has to work." He was respected by the Miao as a master craftsman and musical genius. Each morning at sunrise he went into the neighboring forest to collect bamboo. Using the varying lengths of bamboo, he fashioned musical instruments, which he called *lusheng*. In the afternoons he helped assemble the amazing musical instruments and taught the Miao how to play. The festival was scheduled to be held on the second full moon after the winter solstice. Miao came from all over Guizhou to take part in the festivities. Feasting, singing, dancing, and *lusheng* playing lasted for three days. The melodies of the *lusheng* were carried on the wind and the resonant sounds filled the village and surrounding forest with music. Late on the third night Maosa appeared.

Immediately he was taken to Ahwong's house by the surprised and delighted villagers. The young hunter did not understand the reason for all the excitement. He was very confused. Ahwong's father began questioning him, "Where did you get the white feather that you wear in your hat?"

Maosa related the story, but still did not know the celebration had been held in his honor. Ahwong's father revealed the reason for the festival and led Maosa to meet his daughter.

This meeting was their first, but when Maosa and Ahwong saw one another they were sure of their love. Fate had already entwined their hearts and now their lives were joined together forever. The Miao played

their *lusheng*s long into the night, and dancing and feasting continued until dawn to celebrate Maosa and Ahwong's happiness.

As the sun rose in the east, Ahwong's father set down his *lusheng* and recommended that each year a Lusheng Festival be held to welcome in the New Year, to ensure an abundant harvest, and to let the Miao find their true love. He ended the first festival by inserting a piece of straw in the middle of the field where the celebration had taken place. "Now it is time to get back to planting," he said.

As the Miao left the festival to return to their planting, many could be seen wearing white feathers in their hats. Ever since that time, the custom of wearing a feather has continued. It symbolizes good luck, good fortune, and, more important, true love.

THE Lusheng Festival has been celebrated each year by the Miao people ever since that time so long ago. The date of the festival is the beginning of spring on the lunar calendar, and it is held sometime during January or February, the same date that the Han celebrate the New Year, or "Spring Festival." Miao men and women wear their colorfully embroidered traditional clothing to welcome the Lusheng Festival. The celebration also includes special foods in anticipation of a bountiful harvest that will surely be a part of their coming year. They honor this festival with dancing, singing, and, of course, playing the *lusheng*.

Music of the *lusheng* is as ancient as the instrument itself. The instrument is made of hollow bamboo reeds of assorted lengths tied together with a common mouthpiece, and it is played at Miao festivals and accompanies singing and dancing. Many legends surround the origins of the *lusheng*, including the story of Maosa and Ahwong. These stories are widely known, discussed, and debated by the Miao. Like all retold stories, they can change over the years and from place to place depending on the storytellers.

The *lusheng* accompanies the dances in which young and old participate. Dances are performed in circles, and the size of the circles depends upon the number of people that join—sometimes whole villages take part. Dancers shuffle their feet slowly in a forward motion, taking small steps and using graceful hand movements as they circle counterclockwise. Circles form within circles and the oldest members of the village are shown respect by being placed in the middle.

Miao festivals not only show respect by honoring the elders in the villages, but also the elders honor the people by sharing the traditional folktales in their Miao language. There are three main Miao dialects spoken today, but no written language is in use. According to a legend, the Miao once had a written language, but it was lost when they crossed a large river. Speaking Miao is one way of passing down oral traditions and folktales from generation to generation to keep the distinctive Miao heritage vibrant.

Culture for the Miao is also kept alive by the people wearing their traditional dress. For the festivals Miao men also dress quite colorfully often wearing thickly wrapped headdresses and wrapping embroidered sashes around their waists.

Many Miao girls learn batik, embroidery, and cross-stitch when they are very young—five or six years old. As they mature and perfect these arts, their intricate designs and patterns become true works of art. These designs include dragons, flowers, birds, insects, human forms, and geometric patterns, reflecting a love for nature and the environment. These colorful and bold patterns are embroidered on their blouses, skirts, bags, and belts. In the countryside, Miao girls begin their wedding dresses at an early age because they take a long time to complete. For some groups of Miao, the long skirt of the wedding dress is pleated to resemble a peacock's tail. There is an old story about a Miao man who captures a peacock, which turns out to be his true love. In many Miao villages, a girl's status comes from her skills with a needle and in designing a wedding dress.

Designing clothes to be worn for celebrations and festivals is important because the colorful creations allow prospective sweethearts a time to be noticed, become acquainted, and possibly find a spouse. Many of the young people keep the custom of wearing a feather in their headdresses or hats to bring them good luck and, more important, to bring them love. This custom began with the story of Maosa and Ahwong, and today in the countryside you can see Miao wearing feathers made of highly polished silver instead of the traditional bird feather.

A Legend of Ni Chi

THE STORY OF THE HANI NEW YEAR FESTIVAL

ONCE upon a time in an isolated area of Yunnan, high on the wooded slopes of the Ailao Mountains, lived a kind and diligent Hani farmer known as Ni Chi. His small village of Wunipuka was nestled in the fold of the velvet green mountains and was blessed with rainfall most of the year. Every day Ni Chi farmed the terraced fields on the steep hillsides in order to grow enough food to feed himself and his parents. Like all Hani men, Ni Chi honored his father and mother and took very good care of them. Each day, after working in the fields, he prepared meals of hot soup and rice and served his parents their bowls with two hands to show them the respect they deserved.

One day on his way back from the fields Ni Chi saw in the distance something that looked like a dark cloud looming over the horizon. It got bigger and bigger until the black, whirling mass covered the entire sky. The thunderous wind that surrounded it seemed to explode in the air and to destroy everything in its path. Ni Chi tried to run for cover, but there was no place to hide. Just when he thought he would be swept up and torn to bits—the wind ceased.

As the dust settled he could see that directly in his path lay a man who had been dashed to the ground. "Help me, help me," the crumpled man moaned and pleaded. Ni Chi, being kindhearted, helped him to his feet and said, "Poor stranger, there are ninety-nine roads on the earth, but you didn't come on any of them. There are ninety-nine rivers that flow through

the mountains, but you didn't come on any of them. Did you really come on the wind?"

The pitiful-looking stranger, with tears streaming down his weathered face, began, "Yes, young man. While I was walking along the path, a whirling blackness picked me up and carried me here. My body and bones have been scattered. I'm a woodchopper from a village high in the mountains. How will I ever get back home?"

After hearing his sad story, kind Ni Chi felt sorry for the stranger and invited him home. Ni Chi lit a fire to prepare a simple meal of rice and hot water. Before the blackness of night fell upon the village, Ni Chi made a bed of straw for the stranger so that his guest could rest. During the night a chill wind blew through the cracks in the mud walls, and Ni Chi worried that the man might not have enough clothes to keep warm. Just past midnight Ni Chi lit a candle and climbed down from the loft to check on his guest, but when he looked the bed was empty!

Eerie sounds came from his parents' room, and Ni Chi forced himself to look through the crack. Silver streaks of moonlight illuminated the shocking scene. Standing in the center of the room was a gigantic, blue-eyed monster with fresh, ruby-red blood dripping from its long, white fangs. Ni Chi's parents lay in a heap on the blood-stained earthen floor. At once he knew that he had invited a monster into the house. Overcome with fear and grief, Ni Chi looked down at his bare hands. "How can I fight such a creature with only these?" he wept.

The monster heard the weeping and instantly turned toward the door. Quickly Ni Chi hid under a large, wooden rice barrel that stood by the fireplace. "You will never escape," the monster howled. "NEVER!"

Hiding under the barrel, Ni Chi thought to himself, "I can't wait here to be caught. I have to avenge my parents' death." For what seemed like an eternity he listened for the monster, but everything was quiet. Finally Ni Chi decided to try his luck and escape. Carrying the large, wooden

barrel he ran as fast as his legs could take him to the Red River. When he reached the safety of the river, he placed the barrel on the flowing water and crawled inside.

For three days Ni Chi floated along on the scarlet-colored currents of the wide river. On the morning of fourth day he heard a high-pitched wailing from the riverbank, where a woman sat in sorrow. "Dear woman," he called out to her from his barrel, "Your tears have caused the River God to take notice. Do you see that you have stopped the water from flowing?"

"I can't stop crying," she sobbed. "Yesterday my daughter, Jasmine, and I were planting golden beans when all of a sudden a violent windstorm came upon us. It swept through our garden. Then, as if by magic, a handsome young man appeared. He asked me if I would let him marry my daughter."

"How did you answer?" Ni Chi asked.

"I told him that I needed him to stay with us so that I could get to know his manner and behavior. If he fit my requirements, then, of course, I would satisfy his request. I also explained that a trellis is necessary when you plant beans so that they have something to cling to. It is the same with a husband and a wife."

"And what did he say to that?" Ni Chi asked.

"He called me many hateful names and said that he would take my daughter with or without my permission. Then suddenly a violent wind came up and my daughter disappeared." The old woman began weeping again.

When her tears finally subsided she told Ni Chi about a dream she had the previous night. "Last night while I slept a vision shaped like a cloud appeared and said, 'Tomorrow wait by the river and a young man who will be your son-in-law will come to save your daughter.' That is why I'm waiting here. Also the dream told me that a magic sword is in the swirling, spinning center of the river, and the man must find the sword to kill the monster."

After listening to her story Ni Chi knew that the same monster that had stolen her daughter had also killed his parents. He was determined to find the sword and destroy the monster before it could cause any more harm.

Finding the sword was easy because it was located exactly where the old woman's dream had said, at the whirling, twirling center of the river. Getting it would be difficult because the center was the most turbulent part—the most chaotic. Several times Ni Chi saw the gleaming sword, but he could not reach it. On his last try he fell out of the barrel and almost drowned, but before he was pulled under by the surging current he managed to grasp the sword and eventually swim to safety.

Armed with the magic sword, Ni Chi started on his journey to find the monster. Just before he set out, the old woman told him that he would know her daughter when he saw a beautiful young woman with a black

mole on the palm of her hand. Then the old woman took one of her silver bracelets from her wrist and handed it to Ni Chi. "Please show this to her when you meet," the mother said. "This way she will know you."

After traveling ninety-nine roads and crossing ninety-nine rivers, Ni Chi finally came upon the monster. Ni Chi recognized the monster immediately even though the monster was disguised, this time, as a gentle looking maiden. At the same instant the monster knew that Ni Chi had come to destroy him, but he could not get close to Ni Chi because of the power of the magic sword.

The monster-maiden quickly devised a plan and asked, "Kindhearted brother, would you please deliver this letter to my home?"

"I'll deliver the letter," Ni Chi answered. He knew it was a trick, but he wanted to find Jasmine, the old woman's daughter. He also felt confident because he had the magic sword to protect him.

Ni Chi walked and walked until he became so tired that he finally had to sit down to rest. He found a large, flat rock and stretched out in the warm sun to take a nap. While he slept he dreamed. In his dream appeared an old peasant woman who told him to feed a centipede to the monster in order to kill him. As if by magic, when Ni Chi awoke he found a twelve-inch, black centipede right by his foot. Carefully he picked up the centipede, gingerly wrapped it in his handkerchief, and then started toward his destination.

Soon he came upon the house that the monster-maiden had described. A house with a pointed, thatched roof built on stilts that stood on the outskirts of the village. He walked up the uneven plank steps and knocked on the door. No answer. He waited. He knocked again. Finally the door opened, and standing in the doorway was the loveliest young woman he had ever seen. "I have a letter for you," Ni Chi said, while extending the letter with his two hands.

As the gentle looking young woman with downcast eyes took the letter from his hands, he could see a black mole on her palm. Now he was sure this was Jasmine.

After reading the letter she invited him inside. The letter ordered her to poison Ni Chi, and her fear of the monster made her obey. As is the custom in all Hani homes, she offered Ni Chi a cup of rice wine, but in this cup she placed a small amount of poison. When Ni Chi reached up to take the wine, Jasmine saw the silver bracelet on his arm. Recognizing it as her mother's jewelry, she dropped the cup, spilling the poisoned wine onto the floor.

Instantly Jasmine burst into tears and begged Ni Chi for his forgiveness. At once he forgave her and went on to explain what had happened and why he had come. Together they decided on a plan to destroy the monster.

Early the following day the monster returned home. He became very angry when he saw that Ni Chi was still alive. In order to kill Ni Chi, the monster needed Jasmine's help. Putting a sweet smile on his face, the monster whispered softly to Jasmine, "For your own safety, my dear, I'll have to kill the visitor. But you'll have to help me. You have to get his sword away from him."

"Oh, getting his sword will be easy," Jasmine said, pretending she would help. "Don't worry about the sword. That can wait. Let me prepare some delicious food for you. You must be very hungry."

She prepared all the mouth-watering food that the monster liked, and inside the *baba,* or flat bread, his favorite, she stuffed the black centipede. After eating the *baba,* the monster fell to the ground, clutching his stomach and rolling around. The deadly centipede poison worked quickly. Soon the monster became weak, and with one blow from Ni Chi's enchanted sword the monster lay dead.

Having killed the horrid monster and having avenged his parents' death, Ni Chi and Jasmine returned to his village. On the walk back to the village Jasmine could see and appreciate Ni Chi's qualities: his gentle,

genuine, gallant, gracious, and generous behavior. Jasmine recognized what kind of person he was and all he had done for her, and she gave him her colorful, embroidered belt. When a Hani woman gives her embroidered belt to a man, it shows that she is also giving her heart. A gesture of love.

Upon their return the villagers held a big feast to welcome Ni Chi and Jasmine. Because it was also the Hani New Year, the two celebrations were combined. Table after table of delicious Hani food was lined up one after the other. These tables began in the center of the village and continued for more than two *li,* about one mile, in both directions. While the village elder sampled the food, Ni Chi and Jasmine took their turn on the bamboo swing that was set up near the center of the village.

Ever since that time the legend of Ni Chi has been told and retold until it has become a part of the Hani New Year Festival. In Hani villages along the Red River, people still gather together each year to celebrate the story of the sweethearts, to set up bamboo swings, and to send out the old year and welcome in the new one.

HOW THE HANI NEW YEAR FESTIVAL IS
NOW CELEBRATED

ACH year, on the first day of the tenth month of the Hani lunar calendar, the Hani people celebrate a New Year Festival to welcome in the New Year, celebrate the autumn harvest, and retell the story of Ni Chi. The Hani have many different names for the festival depending on the different areas in which they live, but the festivals are celebrated in similar ways.

Chickens are often sacrificed to honor a special spirit: a mountain spirit, river spirit, or forest spirit. These sacrifices are made to appease the gods and to ensure that the cycle of the seasons continue.

All the families prepare their most delicious food, and early in the morning they take the dishes to the center of town so that the village elder may taste them. Bamboo shoots are a favorite food to be eaten because symbolically they suggest the harvest will be as bountiful as the many bamboo shoots that sprout from the "parent" plant after a rain. As soon as the village elder finishes tasting all the food, the dishes are arranged on tables along the street. Sometimes these tables of food extend for a mile or more.

In many villages along the Red River, the Hani continue the traditional week-long celebrations, giving families the opportunity to travel long distances to visit one another. The New Year is also the time for matchmaking, and young couples are introduced to each other by go-betweens who arrange their marriages. The romantic legend of Ni Chi and Jasmine is still talked about at the New Year Fesitval, and just like Ni Chi and Jasmine the new couples take their turns on the village swing.

In, or near, the center of the village a bamboo frame is constructed and a swing is tied to a frame. Sometimes several swings are suspended from multiple bamboo frames fixed together—resembling a Ferris wheel. The ritual of the swing is important for young and old alike. The Hani believe that swinging sends the bad luck away and encourages good luck to come.

During the festival the Hani women wear their finest clothing, which usually consists of dark cotton robes or tops with long pants or leggings. The edges of their clothing are decorated with brilliant embroidery, gaily colored tassels, and small, dangling silver balls. Shimmering silver jewelry adorns the Hani women, and few are seen without earrings, necklaces, and bracelets. Pieces of jade and silver were once sewn on their close-fitting caps, but recently the jade and silver ornaments have been replaced by shiny scrap metal or caps from soda bottles. Hani men do not dress as colorfully as the women, but many still wear the traditional turbans fashioned of black or white fabric.

The Hani are a very social and generous people and they treat outsiders with great respect. If you visit a Hani village during a festival, you will be in for a treat. It is quite likely that you will sample unusual and delicious food, take a turn on the swing, and be invited into homes for a bowl of wine or a glass of hot tea. To refuse an invitation would bring shame to the Hani village.

Photo by Huang Qi

CAROLYN HAN has been fascinated with China from an early age, and in 1981 she finally had the opportunity to visit. For six weeks she traveled to many interesting places and realized that she wanted to return. In 1985, after receiving her M.A. in English from San Diego State University, she taught English at Chongqing University in Sichuan Province for one year. Her desire to learn more about China and the minority people made her stay another two years in Kunming at Yunnan Institute of the Nationalities. After returning to Hawai'i she wanted to share her China experiences and began by retelling folktales from the minority groups.

She is a lecturer at Hawai'i Community College during the academic year and spends summers in China collecting folktales and researching the different minorities. Her fascination with China has not diminished over the years; it has grown stronger.

As Chinese Studies Associate with the University of Hawai'i at Mānoa and a guest speaker for Pacific and Asian Affairs Council, she has the opportunity to promote international awareness in our shrinking world.

ABOUT THE TRANSLATOR

Photo by Huang Qi

JAY HAN was born in Shanghai, and shortly afterward his family moved to Kunming, Yunnan, where he grew up. He was educated at Yunnan Teacher's College, and taught English for several years in China. Currently he is working in private industry in Yunnan.

He has a deep understanding and love for his country, together with a great interest in sharing his cultural heritage with others in the world. His hope is that people will see the beauty of the Chinese culture and want to know more.

ABOUT THE ILLUSTRATOR

Photo by Huang Qi

Lı Jı was born in Kunming, Yunnan Province. He graduated from Sichuan Fine Art Institute in Chongqing in 1987 and completed an advanced degree in printmaking in 1990.

Currently Li Ji teaches in the Fine Arts Department of Yunnan Art Institute and is a member of China's Print Association. His paintings have won many awards, including the Creative Work Prize of China's Youth Printmaking Exhibition, and have been exhibited in Hong Kong, Taiwan, and the United States. His art has been featured in publications in China and in Taiwan).

His first book to be published in the United States, *Why Snails Have Shells: Minority and Han Folktales of China*, received the Rounce & Coffin Club Award for 1994, which includes exhibition in more than thirty public and academic libraries in the United States during a two-year tour. It also received the Ka Palapala Poʻokela Award for Excellence in Illustration for 1995 from the Hawaii Book Publishers Association.